Little Bear Sleeping

by Tony Johnston

illustrated by Lillian Hoban

G. P. Putnam's Sons New York

Text copyright © 1991 by Tony Johnston
Illustrations copyright © 1991 by Lillian Hoban
G. P. Putnam's Sons, a division of The Putnam & Grosset Book Group,
200 Madison Avenue, New York, NY 10016.   Published simultaneously in Canada.

Library of Congress Cataloging-in-Publication Data
Johnston, Tony.   Little bear sleeping / by Tony Johnston:
illustrated by Lillian Hoban.   p.   cm.
Summary: In this story told in verse, a yawning bear
tries to convince his mother that it isn't time for bed.
[1. Bedtime—Fiction.   2. Bears—Fiction.   3. Stories in rhyme.]
I. Hoban, Lillian, ill. II. Title.   PZ8.3.J639L1 1991
[E]—dc19   89-3796   CIP   AC
ISBN 0-399-22157-3
1   3   5   7   9   10   8   6   4   2
First Impression

For my dear Sara and David Brant
— TJ

For Benjamin, my little bear
—LH

There is a little bear yawning
in a house in a hill,
while the stars shine so still.
There is a little bear yawning.

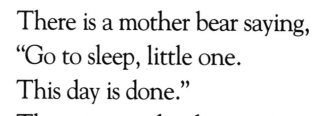

There is a mother bear saying,
"Go to sleep, little one.
This day is done."
There is a mother bear saying.

"I am not sleepy, Mother.
I want to stay up
and drink milk from a cup.
I am not sleepy, Mother."

There is a mother bear smiling.
"Not sleepy at all?"
"I want to play ball."
There is a mother bear smiling.

There is a little bear playing,
with a bat and a ball
and his little bear doll.
There is a little bear playing.

There is a yellow moon rising
by itself in the sky,
so quiet and high.
There is a yellow moon rising.

There is a little bear yawning
on a rug by the fire,
while the moon rises higher.
There is a little bear yawning.

There is a mother bear saying,
"Go to sleep, little one.
This day is done."
There is a mother bear saying.

"I am not sleepy, Mother.
I'll count each little light
in the big, black night.
I am not sleepy, Mother."

There is a little bear counting.
"One million and none.
One million and one."
There is a little bear counting.

There is a little bear yawning.
"One million and ten.
I will count them again."
There is a little bear yawning.

There is a mother bear whispering
in a big rocking chair.
She is telling of bears.
There is a mother bear whispering.

There is a little clock ticking.
Go to sleep, little bear,
in your big rocking chair.
There is a little clock ticking.

There is a little bear rocking
in a mother bear's lap,
in a little nightcap.
There is a little bear rocking.

There is a little bear sleeping
in a house in a hill,
while the stars shine so still.
There is a little bear sleeping.